Julia Donaldson
David Roberts

TYRANNOSAURUS DRIP

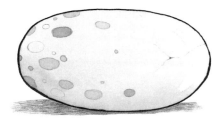

A FEIWEL AND FRIENDS BOOK
An Imprint of Macmillan

Library of Congress Cataloging-in-Publication Data Available

ISBN-13: 978-0-312-37747-2
ISBN-10: 0-312-37747-9

Feiwel and Friends logo designed by Filomena Tuosto

First published in the United Kingdom by Macmillan Children's Books, a division of Pan Macmillan.

First published in the United States by Feiwel and Friends, an imprint of Macmillan.

First U.S. Edition: June 2008

10 9 8 7 6 5 4 3 2 1

www.feiwelandfriends.com

Julia Donaldson
David Roberts

TYRANNOSAURUS DRIP

FEIWEL AND FRIENDS
NEW YORK

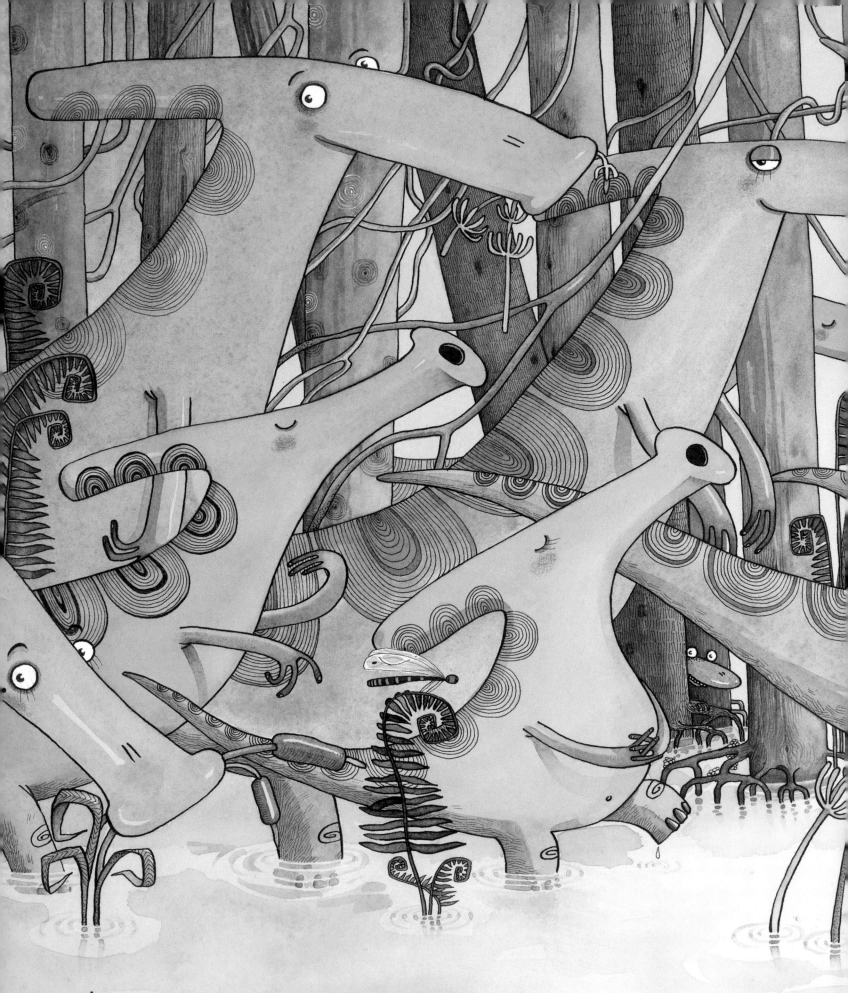

In a prehistoric river in a prehistoric swamp,

Lived a herd of duckbill dinosaurs who liked to stand and chomp.

And they hooted, "Up with rivers!" and they hooted, "Up with reeds!"
And they hooted, "Up with bellyfuls of juicy water weeds!"

Now across the rushy river, on a hill the other side,

Lived a mean Tyrannosaurus with his grim and grisly bride.

And they shouted, "Up with hunting!" and they shouted, "Up with war!"

And they shouted, "Up with bellyfuls of duckbill dinosaur!"

But the two Tyrannosauruses, so grisly, mean, and grim,

Couldn't catch the duckbill dinosaurs because they couldn't swim.

And they muttered, "Down with water!" and they muttered, "Down with wet!"

And they muttered, "What a shame that bridges aren't invented yet."

Now a little Compsognathus (but for short, we'll call her Comp)
Found a duckbill egg and stole it from a nest beside the swamp.

And she swam with it,

And ran with it,

And murmured, "Clever me!"

And, "Won't the baby Comps be thrilled

    With duckbill egg for . . .

"...T!"

She dropped the egg in terror
And went running for her life
From the mean Tyrannosaurus
And his grim and grisly wife.

And the duckbill egg went rolling, and at last it came to rest
In—of all unlikely places—the Tyrannosaurus nest.

Now the mother T had great big jaws

And great enormous legs,

But her brain was rather little

And she couldn't count her eggs.

And she sang, "Hatch out, my terrors,

With your scaly little tails

And your spiky little toothies

And your scary little nails."

Out hatched Babies One and Two,
As perfect as could be,
But Mother T was horrified by
Baby Number Three.
And she grumbled, "He looks weedy,"
And she grumbled, "He looks weak."
And she grumbled, "What long arms—
And look, his mouth is like a beak!"

"He just needs feeding up," said Dad
    And gave the babes some meat.
The first two gulped and guzzled
    But the third refused to eat.
And he said, "I'm really sorry,"
    And he said, "I simply can't."
And he said, "This meat looks horrible.
    I'd rather eat a plant."

"A PLANT!!!" yelled Mom in horror, and Dad said, "Get a grip!"

His sisters found a name for him: "Tyrannosaurus Drip!"

And they shouted, "Up with hunting!" and they shouted, "Up with war!"

And they shouted, "Up with bellyfuls of duckbill dinosaur!"

Poor Tyrannosaurus Drip tried hard to sing along

But the others yelled, "You silly drip, you've got the words all wrong!"

For he hooted, "Down with hunting!" and he hooted, "Down with war!"

And he hooted, "Down with bellyfuls of duckbill dinosaur!"

Drip's sisters soon grew big enough to hunt with Dad and Mom

But they turned on Drip and told him, "You're not fierce enough to come."

And he cried, "They've gone without me," and he cried, "Alackaday!"

And he cried, "This doesn't feel like home. I'm going to run away!"

So he ran off to the river, where he saw a lovely sight:

A herd of duckbill dinosaurs, all hooting with delight.

And they hooted, "Up with rivers!" and they hooted, "Up with reeds!"

And they hooted, "Up with bellyfuls of juicy water weeds!"

As he stood there on the bank, a sudden urge took hold of him,

And he jumped into the water . . . and discovered he could SWIM!

And the duckbills came to greet him by the rushy river's edge

And they hooted, "Nice to see you!" and they hooted, "Have some veg!"

And Drip, who was delighted that they hadn't run away,

Ate bellyfuls of water weeds, and played with them all day.

Then he gazed into the river and he asked them, "Who, oh who

Is that creature in the water?" And they laughed and said, "It's you!"

That night, the lightning crackled
And a storm blew down a tree,

And it fell across the river,
And the Ts cried out, "Yippee!"

And they shouted, "Up with hunting!"
    And they shouted, "Up with war!"
And they shouted, "Up with bellyfuls
    Of duckbill dinosaur!"

Drip's sisters stepped onto the bridge, but then began to frown,

For there in front of them stood Drip, who yelled, "Look out! Look DOWN!"

And they looked into the water, and they each let out a yelp,

And one cried, "Water monsters!" And the other one cried, "HELP!"

Their mother scolded, "Nonsense!"
And she joined them on the tree.
Then she looked into the water and
Exclaimed, "Goodness gracious me!"

The three of them stood trembling, and
Dad said, "Get a grip!
You're all of you as drippy as
Tyrannosaurus Drip!"

He strode onto the bridge
And scoffed,
"I bet there's nothing there."
Then he looked into the water—

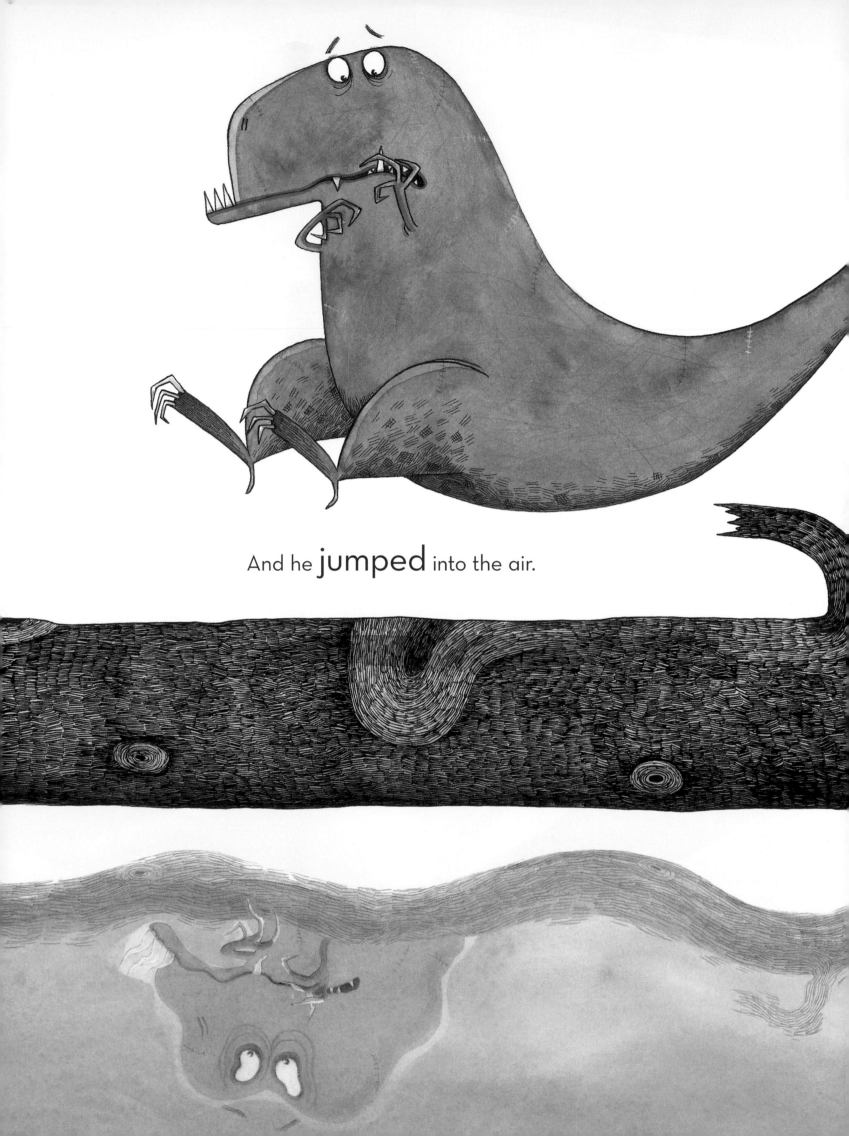

And he **jumped** into the air.

And how the duckbills hooted when he landed with a crash,
And the tree bridge broke . . .

...And four
Tyrannosauruses went

SPLASH!

And spluttering, and clinging to
The branches of the tree,
They went whooshing down a waterfall
And all the way to sea.

And the duckbills hooted happily. They hooted, "Hip hip hip . . .

Hooray for the heroic, one-and-only Duckbill Drip!"

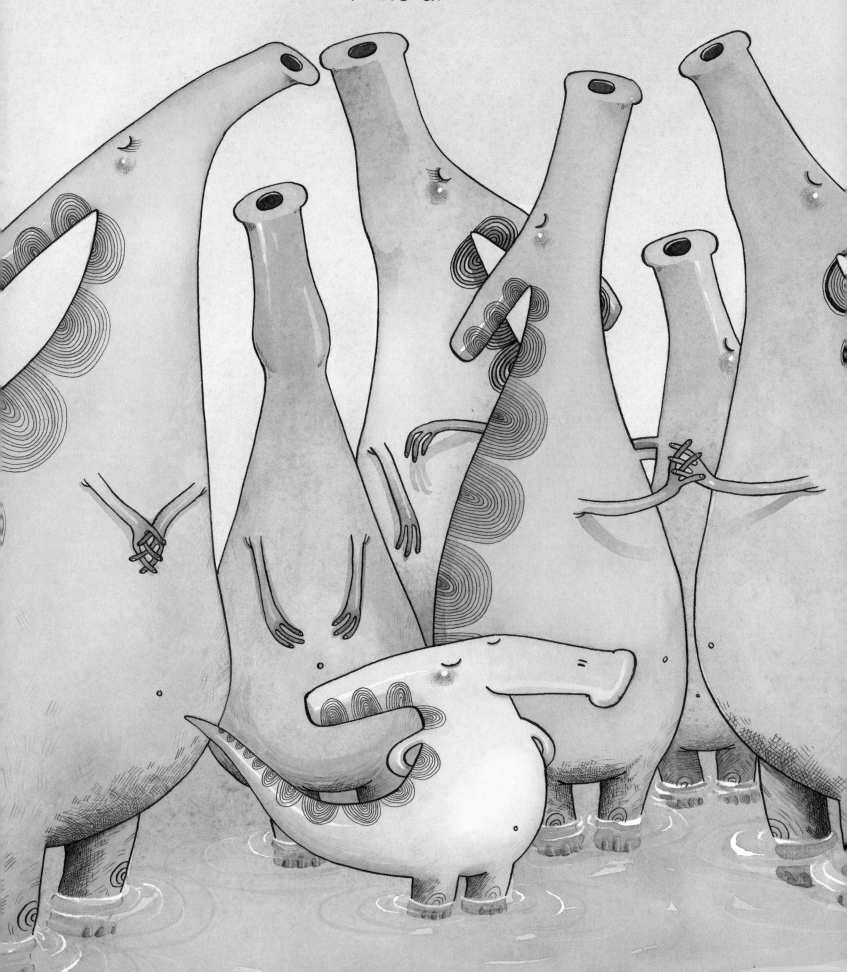